HOW TO BICYCLE TO THE MOON
to plant sunflowers

a simple but brilliant plan in **24** easy steps

MORDICAI GERSTEIN

ROARING BROOK PRESS * * New York

Copyright © 2013 by Mordicai Gerstein
Published by Roaring Brook Press
Roaring Brook Press is a division of Holtzbrinck Publishing Holdings Limited Partnership
175 Fifth Avenue, New York, New York 10010

Library of Congress Cataloging-in-Publication Data

Gerstein, Mordicai.
    How to bicycle to the moon to plant sunflowers : a simple but brilliant plan in twenty-
four easy steps / Mordicai Gerstein.—1st ed.
        p. cm.
    Summary: Too busy with school, soccer, and other activities, a young boy who wants to
cheer up the sad, lonely moon presents the reader with a step-by-step plan for becoming
the first human to bicycle to the moon.
    ISBN 978-1-59643-512-4 (hardcover)
[1. Space flight to the moon—Fiction. 2. Moon—Fiction.] I. Title.
    PZ7.G325Ho 2013
    [E]—dc23
                                                                 2012013787

Roaring Brook Press books are available for special promotions and premiums.
For details contact: Director of Special Markets, Holtzbrinck Publishers.

First Edition, 2013
Printed in China by Toppan Leefung Printing, Ltd., Dongguan City, Guangdong Province
10 9 8 7 6 5 4 3 2 1

How It All Began

THE **FULL MOON** always looked to me like a big, sad clown face.

I asked my parents why it was so sad.

"It's probably lonely," they said. "Nothing lives there."

That's when the idea came to me.

"I'm going to the moon," I said, "to plant sunflowers and cheer it up."

My parents **LAUGHED.**

"How would you get there?" they giggled. "On your bicycle?"

Why **NOT** on my bicycle? With a lot of serious thought, I secretly worked out a plan: **I WOULD BE THE FIRST HUMAN TO BICYCLE TO THE MOON TO PLANT SUNFLOWERS.**

The plan was simple but **BRILLIANT.**

But with homework, soccer, violin, and all the other stuff I had to do, I never had the time to carry it out. That's why I decided to write my plan down so someone else could try it.

MAYBE IT WILL BE YOU!

The Plan

1

OF COURSE, you need a bicycle. I have a red one with three gears and yellow streamers on the ends of the handlebars.

2

NEXT, you need to borrow about *TWO THOUSAND USED TRUCK INNER TUBES.* My Uncle Russell has a tire store. He'd loan them to you.

Have the tubes delivered to a high grassy hill with *TWO TALL, FAT BIRCH TREES* on top of it.

Then get your *best friend* to help you weave the tubes together into **ONE LONG RUBBER BAND**. This should take a couple of weeks. I was going to ask my friend Shirley.

Tie the **ENDS OF THE INNER-TUBE RUBBER BAND** to the **BIRCH TREES**.

Next, get someone with a tractor to **STRETCH THE RUBBER BAND A MILE** down the hill, and *TIE IT TO A HUGE OAK TREE* at the bottom.

You will have made a *GIANT SLINGSHOT!*

Now, you need to find a pole about **25 FEET LONG.** My aunt has a flagpole that would be **PERFECT.**

You also need a **SHIP'S ANCHOR.** Tie the anchor to the top of the pole.

Next, go around your neighborhood asking everyone if they have **OLD GARDEN HOSES.** Most people have lots of them in their garages.

ATTACH ALL THE HOSES together till they're *238,900 MILES LONG* and *WIND THEM ONTO A GIGANTIC SPOOL.*

(238,900 MILES IS THE DISTANCE TO THE MOON!)

Then set the **END OF THE FLAGPOLE** into the **INNER-TUBE SLING-SHOT,** and **TIE THE NOZZLE END** of the **238,900 MILES OF GARDEN HOSE** to the pole.

Wait till the next full moon, **CAREFULLY AIM THE FLAGPOLE** at the moon, and cut the **INNER TUBES** loose. **(THIS SHOULD MAKE A REALLY COOL SOUND!)**

The flagpole will be catapulted into the night sky. Watch it disappear with the hose spinning off the spool after it. Once the flagpole escapes earth's gravity, it will just keep going, **ALL THE WAY TO THE MOON!**

9a While the hose spins off into the sky, write a letter to **NASA**. (That stands for National Aeronautics and Space Agency. **THEY BUILD ROCKETS AND EXPLORE OUTER SPACE!**). It should read something like this:

Dear NASA,

I have a simple but brilliant plan to bicycle to the moon. (Describe the plan.)

Would you please loan me a space suit, size extra small, for a few months? I promise to return it in good condition and give you a full report on my journey.

Yours Truly,

(Your Name)

Now tie your **FAMILY GARDEN HOSE** between the clothesline pole and a tree and start practicing riding your bike on it. If you fall off, *GET RIGHT BACK UP THERE!*

If your parents tell you bicycling on the hose is too **DANGEROUS,** assure them that doing it in outer space will be **SAFER.**

IF YOU FALL YOU JUST FLOAT!

In about three weeks you and your **ENTIRE NEIGHBORHOOD** will hear a **TREMENDOUS** sound.

RUN to the hose spool. If it has **STOPPED SPINNING** and the hose is stretched off into the sky, you'll know your anchor has hit the moon. Tug on the hose. **YOU'LL FEEL THE MOON TUGGING BACK ON THE OTHER END!**

Around this time you will come home from school to hear your mother say, "There's a package for you from . . . **NASA?**"

TEAR OPEN THE PACKAGE. You should find a letter on top:

Dear (Your Name),

We don't know if your plan will work, but it's worth trying. If the enclosed space suit fits, you may borrow it. Good luck!

Sincerely,
NASA

Hopefully, the space suit will fit **PERFECTLY**. At this point your mother will realize your plan is serious and tell you that **YOU CAN'T GO**. Tell her, "Mom . . . I promise I'll be **REALLY** careful!"

"IT'S TOO RISKY!" she'll say, her eyes brimming with tears.

"**PLEASE,** Mom . . . just this once?"

"Well," she'll say, "let me discuss it with your father . . ."

If your parents are like mine . . .

Your mother will *be* sobbing, your father will shake your hand, and everyone else will say *GOOD LUCK AND TAKE CARE.*

14 Start pedaling. In a few minutes, you will *see* your **WHOLE TOWN** below you. Sounds will drift up: screen doors, dogs, lawn mowers, and even scraps of conversations.

If a cloud drifts into your path, **PEDAL RIGHT INTO IT.**
The world will turn white till you come out the other side. As
you get **HIGHER**, you'll probably pass eagles and other birds.
You'll *see* **OCEANS** sparkling far below.

At lunchtime, take a break. Have a peanut butter and jelly sandwich washed down with chocolate milk. **THIS WILL BE YOUR LAST SOLID EARTH FOOD.**

From now on it's all **SPACE FOOD**: nourishing, flavored **GLOP**, squirted through a straw in your space-helmet.

When the sun starts to slide behind the earth, **TRILLIONS** of stars will fill the sky, more than you ever could've imagined. With the moon glowing like a **HUGE NIGHT-LIGHT,** crawl into your sleeping bag. **GET SOME REST.**

Space will be very quiet. The loudest sounds will be your **HEART BEATING,** your **STOMACH GURGLING,** and the **ELECTRIC BUZZING HUM** of your **NERVOUS SYSTEM.** You will sound like a space satellite. You'll see lots of them.

20

FINALLY, you will *see* the pole your hose is tied to, with its anchor stuck into the moon. Pedal down and float off your bike.

YOU WILL BE THE FIRST HUMAN TO BICYCLE TO THE MOON!

Everything will be white except the shadows, which are black. It will look like a coloring book that hasn't been colored yet. You will do amazing **LEAPS** and **SOMERSAULTS.**

21 Take the sunflower seeds and compost out of your pack. Did you remember the trowel? Dig a bunch of **LITTLE HOLES,** put a sunflower seed in each one, and cover it with compost.

Turn on the nozzle of the hose. *(DID YOU REMEMBER TO TURN ON THE FAUCET BEFORE YOU LEFT?)*

The water will come out looking (I think) something like JELL-O. Pat the water onto the compost and mix it in.

That's all there is to it; **YOU'VE PLANTED SUNFLOWERS ON THE MOON!** You might want to gather a few moon rocks as souvenirs for your family and friends.

(22) The **RIDE BACK** will seem **A LOT FASTER**.

I don't Know why, it just **ALWAYS** does on any trip.

When you get back, you will probably be greeted as a **HERO.** There will be **TV CAMERAS, INTERVIEWS,** and all that kind of stuff. The first thing I would want is a **BIG SLICE OF PEPPERONI PIZZA.**

Then just keep **WATERING THE SEEDS** and **WATCHING THE MOON** through your telescope. *I'LL BE WATCHING, TOO.*

And I'm sure that one day, sooner or later, *THANKS TO*
MY PLAN, **WE WILL SEE SUNFLOWERS ON THE MOON!**